People at Work

Working at a Construction Site

by Connor Stratton

FOCUS READERS

SCOUT

www.focusreaders.com

Focus Readers is distributed by North Star Editions:
sales@northstareditions.com | 888-417-0195

Produced for Focus Readers by Red Line Editorial.

Photographs ©: Morsa Images/iStockphoto, cover, 1; Drazen_/iStockphoto, 4; Tempura/iStockphoto, 7; sturti/iStockphoto, 9 (top); monkeybusinessimages/iStockphoto, 9 (bottom); fontgraf/iStockphoto, 11, 16 (bottom left); xaviernau/iStockphoto, 13 (top); bowdenimages/iStockphoto, 13 (bottom), 16 (top left); Air Images/Shutterstock Images, 15; Alexey Slyusarenko/Shutterstock Images, 16 (top right); alexemanuel/iStockphoto, 16 (bottom right)

Library of Congress Cataloging-in-Publication Data
Library of Congress Cataloging-in-Publication Data is available on the Library of Congress website.

ISBN
978-1-64493-013-7 (hardcover)
978-1-64493-092-2 (paperback)
978-1-64493-250-6 (ebook pdf)
978-1-64493-171-4 (hosted ebook)

Printed in the United States of America
Mankato, MN
012020

About the Author

Connor Stratton enjoys building things, eating popcorn, and watching movies with friends. He lives in Minnesota.

Table of Contents

At a Site

Workers go to a
construction site.
They make a building.

Workers wear **helmets**.

Helmets are hard.

Helmets keep heads safe.

helmet

Tools

Workers use many tools.

Workers use **drills**.

Workers use hammers.

drill

hammer

Workers use **cranes**.

Cranes are tall.

Cranes lift things.

crane

Many Parts

Buildings have many parts.

Workers use metal.

Workers use **bricks**.

metal

brick

Workers use wood.
Workers cut the wood
with a saw.

saw
wood

Glossary

bricks

drills

cranes

helmets

Index